T0011869

©2023 Pokémon. ©1995–2023 Nintendo/ Creatures Inc./ GAME FREAK inc. TM, ®, and character names are trademarks of Nintendo.

All rights reserved. Published by Scholastic Inc., *Publishers since 1920.* SCHOLASTIC and associated logos are trademarks and/or registered trademarks of Scholastic Inc.

The publisher does not have any control over and does not assume any responsibility for author or third-party websites or their content.

No part of this publication may be reproduced, stored in a retrieval system, or transmitted in any form or by any means, electronic, mechanical, photocopying, recording, or otherwise, without written permission of the publisher. For information regarding permission, write to Scholastic Inc., Attention: Permissions Department, 557 Broadway, New York, NY 10012.

This book is a work of fiction. Names, characters, places, and incidents are either the product of the author's imagination or are used fictitiously, and any resemblance to actual persons, living or dead, business establishments, events, or locales is entirely coincidental.

ISBN 978-1-339-02652-7

10 9 8 7 6 5 4 3 2   23 24 25 26 27

Printed in the U.S.A.   40
First printing 2023

Designed by Cheung Tai

POKÉMON™

TRIVIA CHALLENGE

QUIZZES, FACTS, AND FUN!

Scholastic Inc.

ARE YOU READY TO DO BATTLE WITH SOME INCREDIBLE QUIZZES?

You'll need your best moves to take on this Trivia Challenge.
Journey across the regions, from Kanto to Galar and beyond, as you face off against more than 300 questions and facts.

There is plenty of research to do and some seriously awesome Pokémon to catch. Each page is packed with trivia that will test your skills as a Trainer, and the pages are ranked for difficulty—just look for the Poké Ball rating!

BONUS AND CHECK OUT THE BONUS MASTER TRAINER QUESTIONS IF YOU CAN HANDLE A CURVEBALL!

LET'S GO, TRAINER!

ALL FIRED UP

Can you identify the Fire-type Pokémon? Peek behind the flames for a clue, then write their number next to their name.

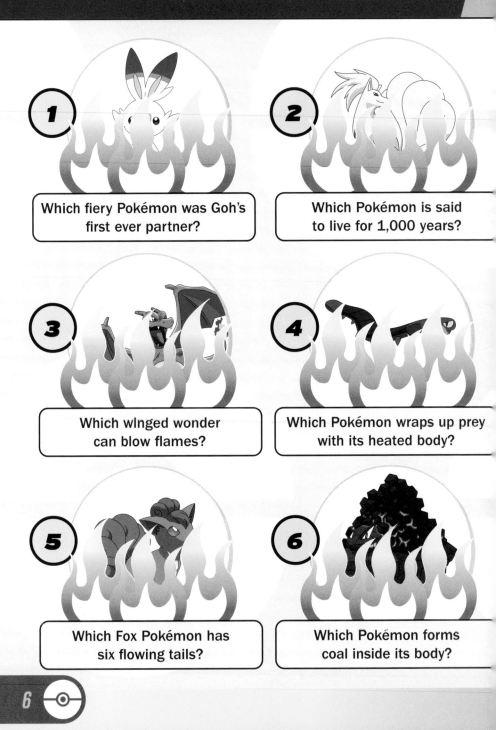

1

Which fiery Pokémon was Goh's first ever partner?

2

Which Pokémon is said to live for 1,000 years?

3

Which winged wonder can blow flames?

4

Which Pokémon wraps up prey with its heated body?

5

Which Fox Pokémon has six flowing tails?

6

Which Pokémon forms coal inside its body?

PICK THE RIGHT POKÉMON

CENTISKORCH ....

CINDERACE ....

NINETALES ....

SCORBUNNY ....

ARCANINE ....

VULPIX ....

SIZZLIPEDE ....

CARKOL ....

CHARIZARD ....

7 Which evolved Pokémon can lash its body like a whip?

8 Which of Goh's Pokémon has a fierce Pyro Ball move?

9 Which agile runner can evolve from a Growlithe?

BONUS **MASTER TRAINER QUESTION** **?** ★ ★ ★ ★ ★

What Fire- and Flying-type Legendary Pokémon from the Johto region is said to live at the foot of a rainbow?

PIKA PIKA QUIZ

How well do you know the Mouse Pokémon?

Try these tricky Pikachu questions.

DIFFICULTY LEVEL:
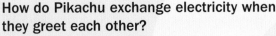

1 How do Pikachu exchange electricity when they greet each other?
a. They rub their cheeks together
b. A high-five zap
c. They touch their tails together

2 What's the shape of a female Pikachu's tail?
a. Lightning bolt
b. Heart
c. Arrow point

3 What object can a Pikachu use to evolve into a Raichu?
a. Water Stone
b. Thunder Stone
c. Sun Stone

4 Which two moves could Ash's Pikachu use in battle?
a. Quick Attack and Draco Meteor
b. Ember and Electroweb
c. Iron Tail and Thunderbolt

5 What type of Pokémon is Pikachu's weakness?
a. Ground
b. Flying
c. Bug

6 What's the correct name of the Pokémon from which Pikachu evolves?
a. Pika
b. Richu
c. Pichu

7 Which Pokémon did Ash's Pikachu battle when it first discovered it could Gigantamax?
 a. Drednaw
 b. Alcremie
 c. Meowth

8 Which Pokémon was Ash training with when Pikachu began to feel a little jealous?
 a. Gengar
 b. Riolu
 c. Dragonite

BONUS *MASTER TRAINER QUESTION* **?** ★ ★ ★ ★ ★

Before Pikachu met Ash, what group of friendly Pokémon did it spend its days with?

HOW DID YOU DO? **TURN TO PAGE 89 TO FIND OUT!**

LET'S PLAY CATCH!

Are you ready to catch some Pokémon in the Kanto region? Read the questions below, then add the correct question number to each of your Pokémon answers on the opposite page.

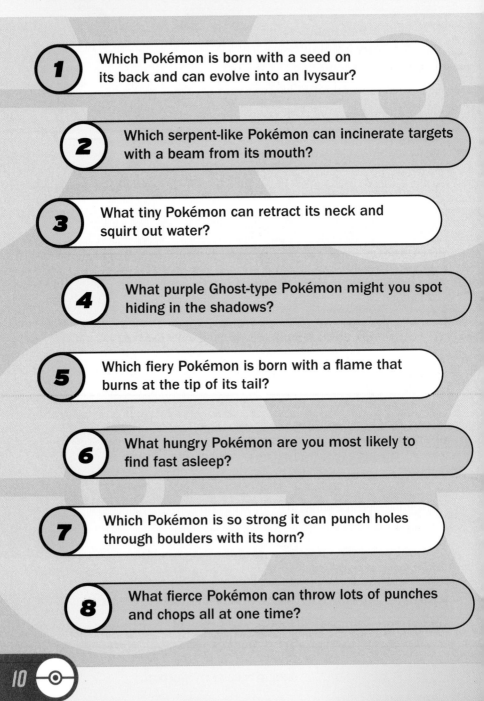

1 Which Pokémon is born with a seed on its back and can evolve into an Ivysaur?

2 Which serpent-like Pokémon can incinerate targets with a beam from its mouth?

3 What tiny Pokémon can retract its neck and squirt out water?

4 What purple Ghost-type Pokémon might you spot hiding in the shadows?

5 Which fiery Pokémon is born with a flame that burns at the tip of its tail?

6 What hungry Pokémon are you most likely to find fast asleep?

7 Which Pokémon is so strong it can punch holes through boulders with its horn?

8 What fierce Pokémon can throw lots of punches and chops all at one time?

MAGIKARP

LAPRAS

BULBASAUR

CHARMANDER

GENGAR

MACHAMP

BUTTERFREE

RHYDON

SNORLAX

GROWLITHE

SQUIRTLE

GYARADOS

HOW DID YOU DO? **TURN TO PAGE 89 TO FIND OUT!**

FACTS

YOU GOTTA KNOW!

EPIC EEVEE

Level up with these fast facts about Eevee!

FACT 1

Eevee is an amazing Pokémon who can evolve into eight different forms that have been discovered so far.

FACT 2

An Eevee met Chloe when it was following Yamper, and they had a special bond from the start.

FACT 3

Chloe chose Eevee to be her very first Pokémon. This is the moment her adventures as a Pokémon Trainer began.

FACT 4

All Eevee possess unstable DNA, which is why they have so many Evolution possibilities.

FACT 5

Chloe's Eevee is totally unique. Researchers at the Eevee Evolution Lab couldn't help it evolve, no matter what stone they used.

FACT 6

Eevee's first fight was against Team Rocket's Pelipper. Together, Yamper and Eevee used Spark to blast it away!

GO ROTOM!

Some Galar region Pokémon have been scrambled in the Pokédex! Answer the questions to fix their files.

1 Which Water-type Pokémon can shoot water from its fingertips?

....

2 Which Pokémon drums rapidly in battle with two wooden sticks?

....

3 Which Pokémon blows sand from its nostrils into opponents' eyes?

....

4 Which Pokémon has dangerous claws that resemble daggers?

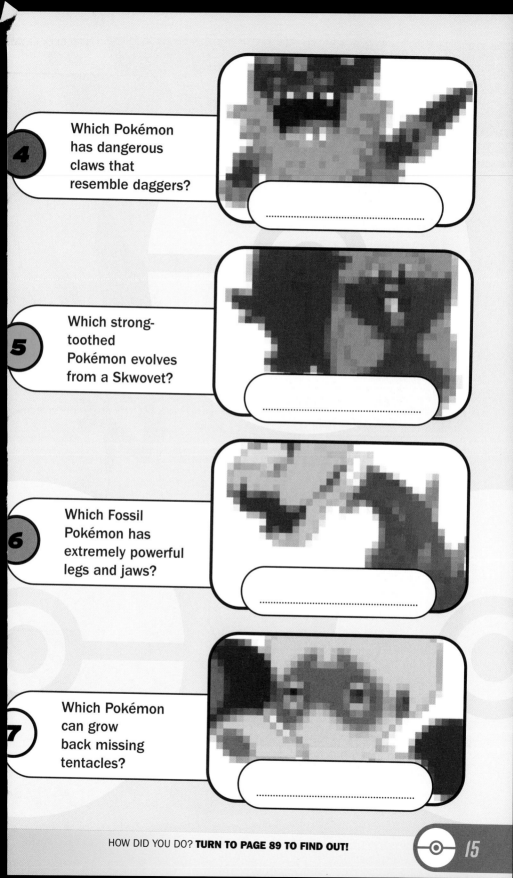

....

5 Which strong-toothed Pokémon evolves from a Skwovet?

....

6 Which Fossil Pokémon has extremely powerful legs and jaws?

....

7 Which Pokémon can grow back missing tentacles?

....

ACE CINDERACE!

Let's hang out with Goh's fierce and loyal partner.
Will these questions leave you scorched?

1 What Pokémon type is Cinderace?

2 In what region did Goh first meet his partner as a Scorbunny?

3 From which Pokémon does Cinderace evolve?

4 Which Pokémon was Goh battling when his Pokémon evolved to a Cinderace?

5 What is the name of Cinderace's fireball-kick move?

6 Which teammate did Goh's Cinderace often comfort when it cried?

MAP THE WAY

Ash and Goh have traveled across the map in search of new Pokémon. Can you name all the regions they visited?

1 Ash is from Pallet Town, but in what region is it?

K _ N _ _ _

2 In which region did Ash and Goh first encounter a Suicune by a lake?

J O _ _ _ _

3 In which region did the heroes rescue Lavaridge Town's hot springs?

_ _ E _ N

4 Where have Ash and Goh visited the fiery hot Desert Resort?

U N _ _ _ _

5 Mount Coronet is in which region?

_ I _ _ O _

6 In which region is the Castle of Chivalry training facility?

K _ _ _ _ S

7 Where did Goh catch an Exeggutor on his first visit?

_ _ _ _ _ A

8 Where is the Wild Area where Ash and Goh discovered Dynamax Pokémon?

_ A _ _ _ _

ODD POKÉMON OUT

Which Pokémon does not belong? Circle your choice for each question.

DIFFICULTY LEVEL:

Which of these Pokémon is *not* from the Galar region?
a. Nickit
b. Gengar
c. Grookey

Which Pokémon does *not* have wings?
a. Pidgeot
b. Charizard
c. Falinks

Which Pokémon does *not* evolve?
a. Lapras
b. Joltik
c. Gossifleur

Which Pokémon is *not* a dual type?
a. Gastly
b. Grimmsnarl
c. Grubbin

Which Pokémon does *not* have a tail?
a. Boldore
b. Charmeleon
c. Lucario

6 Which Pokémon is *not* a Psychic type?
a. Mew
b. Indeedee
c. Ninetales

7 Which Pokémon is *not* fully evolved?
a. Garchomp
b. Geodude
c. Grapploct

8 Which Pokémon is *not* black and white?
a. Galarian Linoone
b. Galarian Yamask
c. Galarian Zigzagoon

BONUS **MASTER TRAINER QUESTION** **?** ★ ★ ★ ★ ★

Which Dark- and Dragon-type Pokémon has not one, but two heads?

FACTS
YOU GOTTA KNOW!

FARFETCH'D FACTS

Get training with the awesome Galarian Farfetch'd!

FACT 1

Galarian Farfetch'd is so strong, it can break rocks with a swipe of its leek!

FACT 2

It is a real warrior, and a key part of its strength is its ability to take a hit.

FACT 3

It has awesome battle moves including Night Slash and Brutal Swing.

FACT 4

Ash's Farfetch'd loves to battle and trained hard to become a Leek Master.

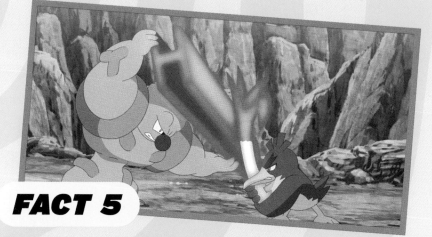

FACT 5

When Ash's Farfetch'd battled against Gurdurr, it shattered Gurdurr's steel beam with a leek smash!

FACT 6

With the help of his Galarian Farfetch'd, Ash jumped up in the Pokémon World Coronation Series rankings.

GALARIAN GAME

Which Pokémon have Galarian forms of previously discovered Pokémon?

Circle your choice each time.

DIFFICULTY LEVEL:

1

FARFETCH'D **OR** ROOKIDEE

2

ARROKUDA **OR** STUNFISK

3

LINOONE **OR** PERRSERKER

4 MR. MIME **OR** MR. RIME

5 MILCERY **OR** RAPIDASH

6 URSHIFU **OR** ZIGZAGOON

7 DARMANITAN **OR** DURALUDON

HOW DID YOU DO? **TURN TO PAGE 90 TO FIND OUT!**

POKÉ BALL PUZZLER!

As you answer the questions below, circle the correct answers on the opposite page.

Which Pokémon is left and has escaped your Poké Ball?

DIFFICULTY LEVEL:

1 Which Fossil Pokémon's mouth is on top of its head?

2 Which drumming Pokémon evolves from Thwackey?

3 Which Pokémon has a shout so loud, opponents wince?

4 Which Pokémon's weapon is also its food?

5 Which cheeky Pokémon thrives on negative energy?

6 Which Pokémon slept for a long time in the form of a statue?

7 Which Pokémon marks its targets with a scent?

8 Which hungry Pokémon can generate electricity?

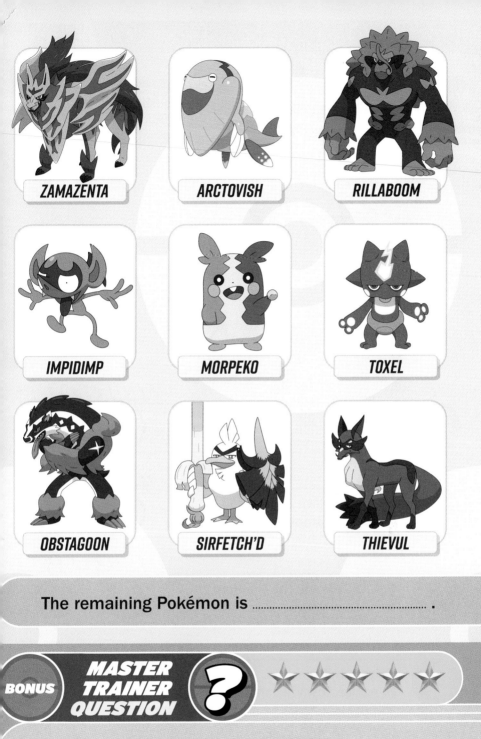

ZAMAZENTA

ARCTOVISH

RILLABOOM

IMPIDIMP

MORPEKO

TOXEL

OBSTAGOON

SIRFETCH'D

THIEVUL

The remaining Pokémon is ....

BONUS **MASTER TRAINER QUESTION** ?

Which of these Pokémon has Boltund as its natural enemy?

TRUE OR FALSE

Are these facts about the Johto region, and the Pokémon discovered there, correct? Mark them true or false.

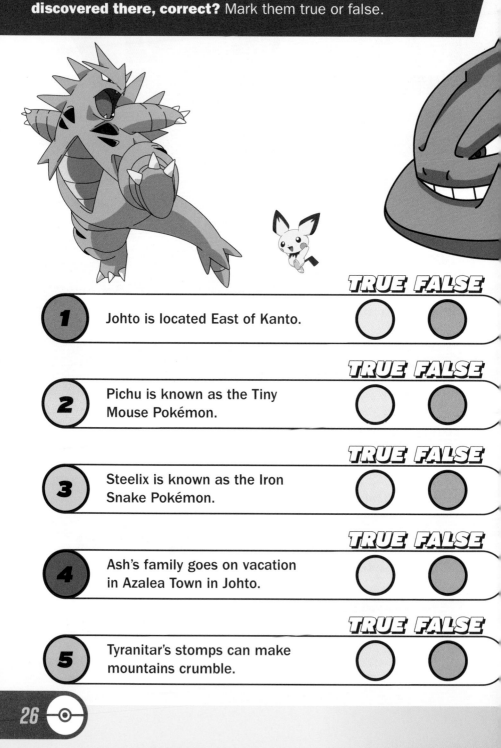

TRUE FALSE

1 Johto is located East of Kanto. ◯ ◯

TRUE FALSE

2 Pichu is known as the Tiny Mouse Pokémon. ◯ ◯

TRUE FALSE

3 Steelix is known as the Iron Snake Pokémon. ◯ ◯

TRUE FALSE

4 Ash's family goes on vacation in Azalea Town in Johto. ◯ ◯

TRUE FALSE

5 Tyranitar's stomps can make mountains crumble. ◯ ◯

TRUE FALSE

6 Goh once caught a Chinchou in Johto.

○ ○

TRUE FALSE

7 When Umbreon becomes angry, it creates an electric charge.

○ ○

TRUE FALSE

8 Ash battled Bea in Johto and the result was a draw.

○ ○

TRUE FALSE

9 Suicune can only survive in water.

○ ○

TRUE FALSE

10 Ho-Oh is a very common sight in Johto.

○ ○

HOW DID YOU DO? **TURN TO PAGE 90 TO FIND OUT!**

EPIC EVOLUTIONS

Which Pokémon is missing in each Evolution chain? Write the missing names in the right spots.

1 BULBASAUR – .... – VENUSAUR

2 SCORBUNNY – RABOOT – ....

3 .... – THWACKEY – RILLABOOM

4 SOBBLE – DRIZZILE – ....

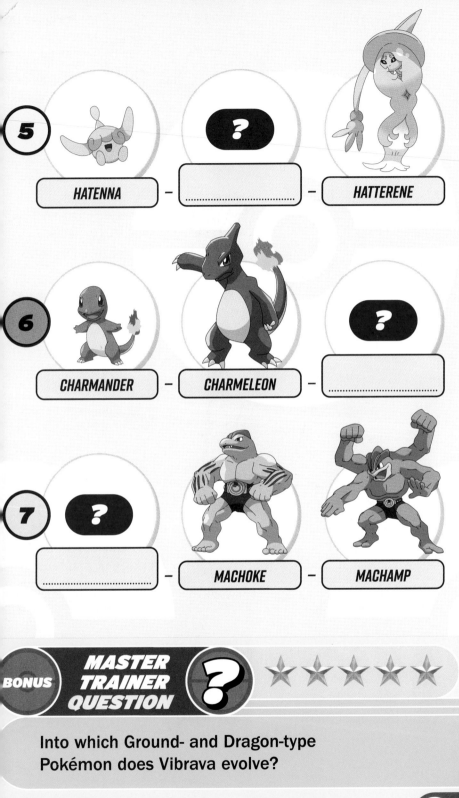

5 HATENNA – .... – HATTERENE

6 CHARMANDER – CHARMELEON – ....

7 .... – MACHOKE – MACHAMP

BONUS **MASTER TRAINER QUESTION** ? ★ ★ ★ ★ ★

Into which Ground- and Dragon-type Pokémon does Vibrava evolve?

FACTS
YOU GOTTA KNOW!

MEGA MOLES

Dig in to these facts about Diglett and Dugtrio!

FACT 1

Diglett gnaw on roots below ground, so they can cause a lot of damage to a harvest.

FACT 2

Diglett hide underground, which makes them difficult to battle or catch!

FACT 3

Dugtrio is the evolved form of Diglett. These three make an excellent team!

FACT 4

When Dugtrio burrows, it loosens the soil and fills it with air, which is great for farming.

FACT 5

Goh caught a Diglett and a Dugtrio when he, Ash, and Chloe were on a mission at Laxton Farm.

FACT 6

When Goh battled with Dugtrio, it used Bulldoze and Sand Tomb moves to blast away Team Rocket!

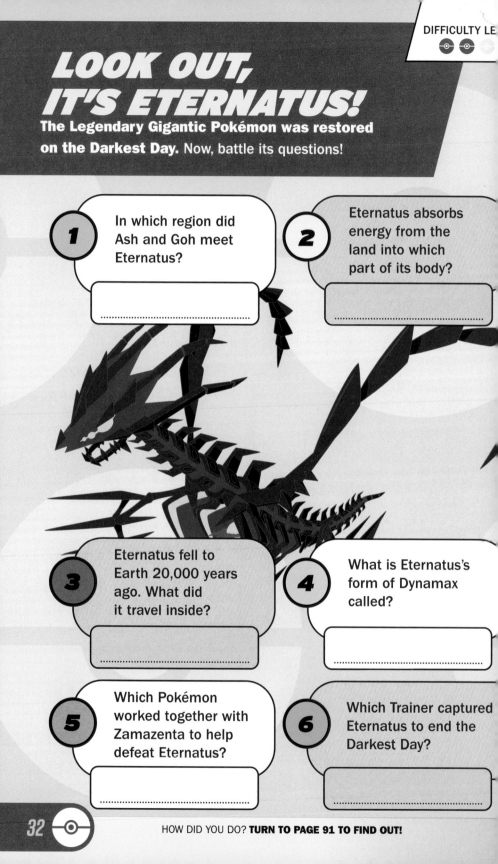

LOOK OUT, IT'S ETERNATUS!

The Legendary Gigantic Pokémon was restored on the Darkest Day. Now, battle its questions!

1 In which region did Ash and Goh meet Eternatus?

....

2 Eternatus absorbs energy from the land into which part of its body?

....

3 Eternatus fell to Earth 20,000 years ago. What did it travel inside?

....

4 What is Eternatus's form of Dynamax called?

....

5 Which Pokémon worked together with Zamazenta to help defeat Eternatus?

....

6 Which Trainer captured Eternatus to end the Darkest Day?

....

HOW DID YOU DO? **TURN TO PAGE 91 TO FIND OUT!**

COLD AS ICE

Pick out the four Ice-type Pokémon below,
then unscramble the letters beside them
to reveal another cool Pokémon!

The hidden Ice-type Pokémon is ___ ___ ___ ___

MEGA MOVES

Can you identify the awesome battle move for each Pokémon?
Write its number next to its name. Here we go!

1 In what move does Blastoise fire powerful blasts of water?

2 What move does Bulbasaur use to lash enemies?

3 In what move does Charizard scorch opponents with an intense blast of heat?

4 What move gives Gengar's opponents a dark fright?

5 What powerful blast from Lucario never misses?

6 What focused move from Garchomp will zap its opponent's energy?

7 In what move does Venusaur launch sharp leaves at its foes?

8 What move does Squirtle use to soak its targets?

CHOOSE THE CORRECT MOVE!

- FLAMETHROWER ....
- AURA SPHERE ....
- HYPER BEAM ....
- WATER GUN ....
- HYDRO PUMP ....
- SHADOW BALL ....
- VINE WHIP ....
- RAZOR LEAF ....

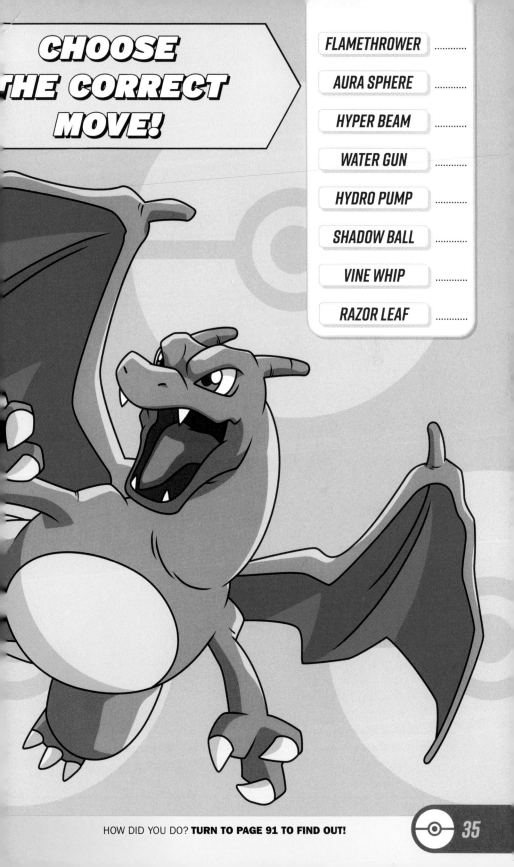

HOW DID YOU DO? **TURN TO PAGE 91 TO FIND OUT!**

CLOSE-UP CLUES

How are your research skills? Name the Pokémon below, using Pokédex close-ups as a hint.

1 Which Pokémon strikes at enemies with jolts of electricity?

2 Which Pokémon can disguise itself as an icicle while it sleeps?

3 Which Larva Pokémon is a lot smarter than it is strong?

4 Which Pokémon attacks by launching electrified fur from its body?

5 Which scorching hot Pokémon has been known to Gigantamax?

6 Which Pokémon's high intelligence is matched by immense psychic power?

7 Which Pokémon can use Stun Spore to paralyze targets?

8 Which icy Pokémon can cause a blizzard to chase away enemies?

9 Which Pokémon hides in its shell as it uses psychic powers?

1 ....

2 ....

3 ....

4 ....

5 ....

6 ....

7 ....

8 ....

9 ....

BONUS **MASTER TRAINER QUESTION** **?** ★ ★ ★ ★ ★

Goh uses a Metal Coat to evolve his Scyther into which Bug- and Steel-type Pokémon?

HOW DID YOU DO? **TURN TO PAGE 91 TO FIND OUT!**

IN THE SHADOWS

Can you match these Dark-type Pokémon facts to their shadow shapes?

Draw a line to connect them.

DIFFICULTY LEVEL:

1 This cunning creature is known as the Fox Pokémon.

a

?

b

2 This Ninja Pokémon has stealthy webbed feet.

3 This Pokémon sucks in negative energy through its nose.

c

?

d

4 This feisty Pokémon moves in zigzags.

5 The Rogue Monkey Pokémon does not evolve.

e

f

6 This loud Pokémon can use its shout to make enemies shudder.

7 This Pokémon uses its long tongue to taunt opponents.

g

h

8 This sly Pokémon can stab targets with its spear-like hair.

FACTS

YOU GOTTA KNOW!

SWEET SUICUNE

Brush up on your knowledge of this Legendary Pokémon!

245

FACT 1

Suicune is a highly respected Legendary Pokémon.

FACT 2

Suicune travels the world purifying polluted water. Once it has cleared a body of water, it moves on.

FACT 3

Ash and Goh once saved a Suicune from Pokémon hunters.

FACT 4

Goh fed Suicune healing berries and bandaged its wounds. They made a very special bond.

FACT 5

Suicune fought alongside Goh and used Hydro Pump to defeat the Pokémon hunters.

FACT 6

Suicune's Ice Beam move can freeze its opponents into an ice block!

BATTLE CHALLENGE!

Get into champion mode with these tough
questions set in the heat of battle.

DIFFICULTY
LEVEL:

When Ash first battled Rinto, which Pokémon
defeated Ash's Farfetch'd?
a. Gallade
b. Geodude
c. Scizor

When Ash and Iris battled in Unova, what
was the lineup of their first challenge?
a. Dracovish vs. Dracovish
b. Haxorus vs. Haxorus
c. Dragonite vs. Dragonite

?

Which Legendary Pokémon did Ash
and Goh battle against with Gary?
a. Moltres
b. Zamazenta
c. Eternatus

?

When Goh tried to catch an Alolan Ninetales,
what move did it use on him?
a. Weather Ball
b. Quick Attack
c. Blizzard

When Goh first met Falinks, which Pokémon
did they battle together?
a. Galarian Stunfisk
b. Eiscue
c. Meowth

6 When Goh was at the Pokémon Catch Adventure Race in Alola, what move did his Pyukumuku use?
a. Toxic
b. Dark Pulse
c. Psychic

7 What move did Pikachu use when he and Ash fought in their first Ultra Class battle against Volkner?
a. Max Steelspike
b. G-Max Volt Crash
c. 10,000 Volt Thunderbolt Z-Move

8 When Ash battled Bea in their Ultra Class battle, which Pokémon beat Bea's Gigantamax Machamp?
a. Pikachu
b. Lucario
c. Grapploct

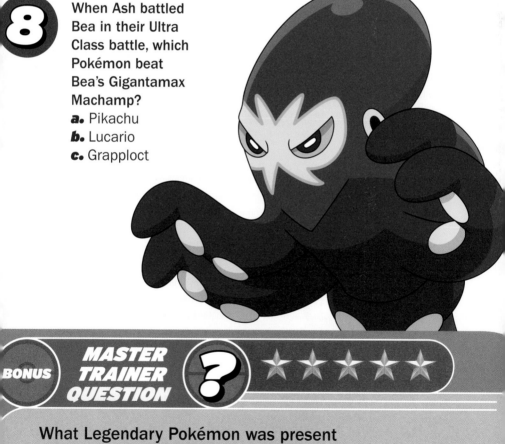

BONUS *MASTER TRAINER QUESTION* **?** ★ ★ ★ ★ ★

What Legendary Pokémon was present the first time Ash and Goh met?

HOW DID YOU DO? **TURN TO PAGE 91 TO FIND OUT!**

MAKE A SPLASH!

Can you catch six Water-type Pokémon?
Circle and name them as you spot them.
Bonus points if you can name the others, too!

DIFFICULTY
LEVEL:

EEVEE EVOLUTIONS

How well do you know the evolved forms of this unique **Pokémon?** Try these questions to find out!

1 What type of weather do you expect when Glaceon is around?

2 Which Evolution of Eevee has an orb on its forehead?

3 What color are Sylveon's paws?

4 What is unusual about Umbreon's sweat?

5 Which Evolution of Eevee can heat air in its internal flame pouch?

6 Which Evolution of Eevee can melt invisibly into water?

7 Which Evolution's fur can bristle like sharp needles?

8 What does it mean when Vaporeon's fins vibrate?

9 Which Evolution of Eevee is a Psychic-type Pokémon?

10 Which Evolution's tail can slice through large trees?

11 What is special about Leafeon's leaves?

12 Which Evolution of Eevee would you call upon to stop conflict?

LET'S GO TO GALAR!

Ash and Goh have made some amazing discoveries in the Galar region. Did you know these fun facts?

FACT 1

Galar is an expansive region, including cities, countryside, and snowy mountains.

FACT 2

Ash and Goh can travel to the Galar region from Vermilion City by train.

FACT 3

The Wild Area in the Galar region is where Ash and Goh discovered Dynamax Pokémon.

FACT 4

When researchers were attempting to restore Fossil Pokémon in the Wild Area, they mixed up the pieces and came up with two odd Pokémon: Dracovish and Arctozolt!

FACT 5

Glimwood Tangle is an enchanted forest where Galarian Ponyta and Galarian Rapidash can be found.

FACT 6

Goh has caught many Pokémon in the Galar region, such as Galarian Stunfisk, Milcery, Morelull, and Sobble.

FACT 7

Ash wanted to compete with Leon since he was the undefeated Champion of the Galar region.

FACT 8

The Galar region has its own form of several Pokémon, such as the Galarian Farfetch'd.

FACT 9

It was in the Galar region that Ash's Riolu evolved into Lucario, and Goh's Raboot evolved into Cinderace.

FACT 10

The "sword" and "shield" from Galar's hero legend are actually Zacian and Zamazenta!

FACTS

YOU GOTTA KNOW!

STEALTHY SOBBLE

This timid Pokémon has some extra-special qualities.

FACT 1

Sobble often cries when it's scared—causing everyone around it to cry, too!

FACT 2

Goh's Sobble learned the U-turn move, where it hits an opponent and quickly runs away.

FACT 3

When Sobble gets wet,
its skin changes color
and it becomes invisible!

FACT 4

Inteleon is Sobble's
final evolved form.

FACT 5

Inteleon is the Secret
Agent Pokémon. It can
shoot water from its
fingers and glide using
a membrane on its back.

FACT 6

Team Rocket once tried
to recruit Inteleon, but it
used Snipe Shot to blast
them away!

WINGED WONDERS

Can you identify these Flying-type Pokémon?

Take a peek at their wings for a clue!

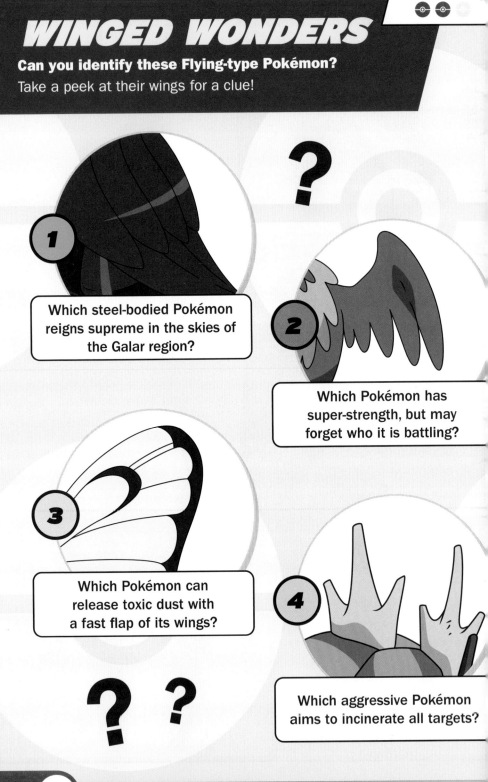

1 Which steel-bodied Pokémon reigns supreme in the skies of the Galar region?

2 Which Pokémon has super-strength, but may forget who it is battling?

3 Which Pokémon can release toxic dust with a fast flap of its wings?

4 Which aggressive Pokémon aims to incinerate all targets?

5 Which Pokémon can spit fire hot enough to melt boulders?

6 Which feathered Pokémon is smart enough to use tools in battle?

7 Which little Pokémon gets stronger with every battle, even a defeat?

1 ....
2 ....
3 ....
4 ....
5 ....
6 ....
7 ....

BONUS **MASTER TRAINER QUESTION** ?

Which Electric- and Flying-type Pokémon has complete control over electricity?

HOW DID YOU DO? **TURN TO PAGE 92 TO FIND OUT!**

NAME THAT TYPE!

Grass, Electric, Fire . . . how well do you know Pokémon types? Circle the correct single or dual types for the Pokémon below.

1 What type is Clobbopus?
a. Water
b. Fighting
c. Ground

2 What type is Drednaw?
a. Water and Rock
b. Dragon and Rock
c. Grass and Rock

3 What type is Applin?
a. Grass
b. Grass and Dragon
c. Grass and Bug

4 What type is Grimmsnarl?
a. Psychic and Dark
b. Dark
c. Dark and Fairy

5 What type is Barraskewda?
a. Grass
b. Water
c. Dragon

6 What type is Greedent?
a. Normal
b. Ground
c. Dark

7 What type is Cufant?
a. Ice
b. Rock
c. Steel

8 What type is Toxtricity?
a. Electric and Poison
b. Dark and Poison
c. Ghost and Poison

9 What type is Dragapult?
a. Dragon
b. Dragon and Ghost
c. Dragon and Flying

BONUS **MASTER TRAINER QUESTION** **?** ★ ★ ★ ★ ★

What Normal-type Pokémon is a chatty member of Team Rocket?

GUESS THAT POKÉMON!

Which Kanto region Pokémon is the correct answer to each question? Circle your answers.

1 Which Pokémon's tail becomes deeper in color as it gets older?

a ARCANINE

b RAICHU

c WARTORTLE

2 Which Pokémon stays on the move to seek sunlight?

a VENUSAUR

b SNORLAX

c WARTORTLE

3 Which Pokémon can melt invisibly into water?

a VAPOREON

b MAGIKARP

c KIRLIA

4 Which Pokémon's tongue is made of a deadly gas?

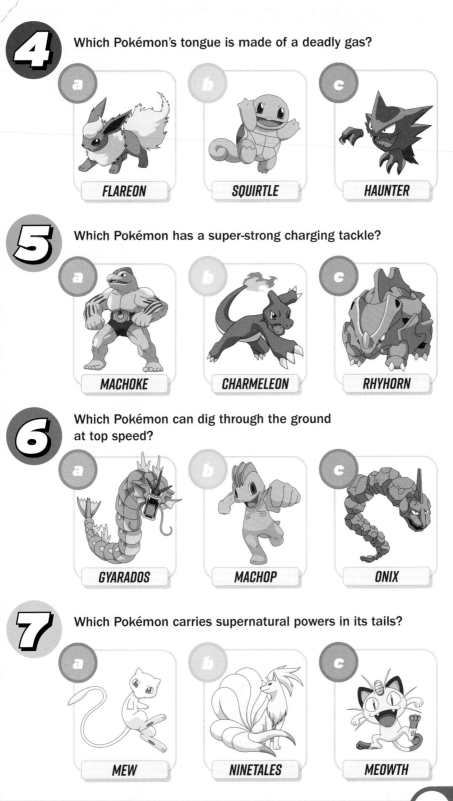

a **FLAREON**

b **SQUIRTLE**

c **HAUNTER**

5 Which Pokémon has a super-strong charging tackle?

a **MACHOKE**

b **CHARMELEON**

c **RHYHORN**

6 Which Pokémon can dig through the ground at top speed?

a **GYARADOS**

b **MACHOP**

c **ONIX**

7 Which Pokémon carries supernatural powers in its tails?

a **MEW**

b **NINETALES**

c **MEOWTH**

HOW DID YOU DO? **TURN TO PAGE 93 TO FIND OUT!**

GET CHARGED UP!

Spark that brain and test yourself with these questions about Electric-type Pokémon!

How many volts of electricity can Toxtricity generate?
a. 5,000
b. 10,000
c. 15,000

Into which body part does Boltund channel its electricity?
a. Tail
b. Legs
c. Ears

What does spiky Pincurchin feed on?
a. Seaweed
b. Vines
c. Rocks

Which Pokémon can be found clinging to other Pokémon?
a. Pikachu
b. Joltik
c. Pincurchin

5 Which Pokémon generates electricity through the shaking of its upper body?
a. Arctozolt
b. Galvantula
c. Charjabug

6 What does Toxel manipulate in its body to create electricity?
a. Water
b. Food
c. Poison

7 Jolteon accumulates negative ions from the atmosphere to do what?
a. To static shock opponents
b. To blast out lightning bolts
c. To help it run super-fast

8 As Yamper runs, where does it generate electricity?
a. The base of its tail
b. The tip of its tongue
c. Under its feet

BONUS *MASTER TRAINER QUESTION* **?** ★ ★ ★ ★ ★

What Bug- and Electric-type Pokémon is the most evolved form of Grubbin?

HOW DID YOU DO? **TURN TO PAGE 93 TO FIND OUT!**

FACTS
YOU GOTTA KNOW!

LET'S GO TO GLIMWOOD

Take a ride with the Galarian forms of Ponyta and Rapidash!

FACT 1

Galarian Ponyta has healing powers in its horn, and it can treat wounds using Heal Pulse.

FACT 2

Galarian Rapidash is Ponyta's evolved form. It is fearless and proud!

FACT 3

Galarian Rapidash uses psychic powers stored in the flowing fur above its hooves to dash through the forest.

FACT 4

Galarian Ponyta and Galarian Rapidash have turned into their unique forms because they have been bathed in the mysterious energy of the forest.

FACT 5

Chloe and Eevee once helped heal a Galarian Rapidash using a special rainbow-colored flower.

FACT 6

Once they bonded, Chloe rode on a Rapidash and Eevee rode on a Ponyta through the forest!

WHO IS EVOLVED?

There are two Pokémon to choose from each time. Which one is the evolved form? Circle the correct answer. Let's go!

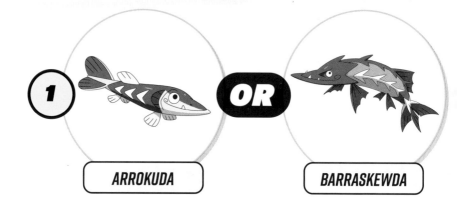

1 ARROKUDA OR BARRASKEWDA

2 ARCANINE OR GROWLITHE

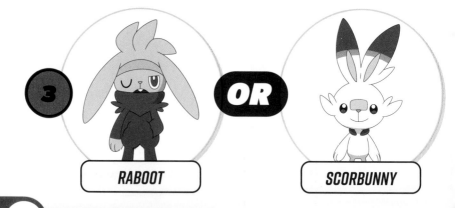

3 RABOOT OR SCORBUNNY

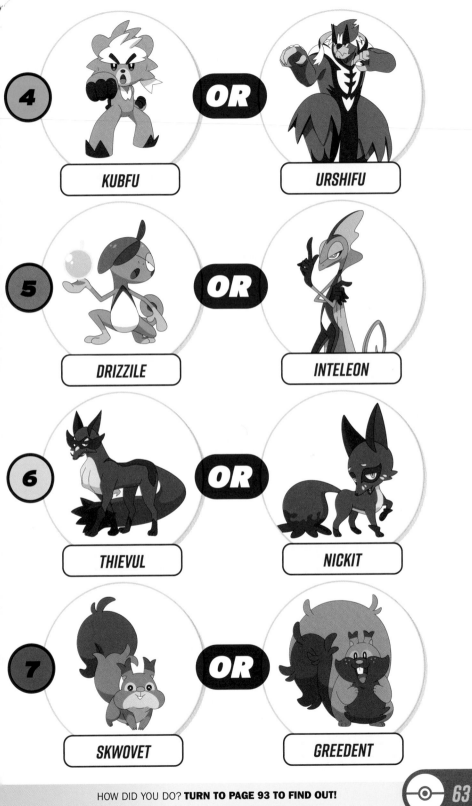

4 KUBFU **OR** URSHIFU

5 DRIZZILE **OR** INTELEON

6 THIEVUL **OR** NICKIT

7 SKWOVET **OR** GREEDENT

HOW DID YOU DO? **TURN TO PAGE 93 TO FIND OUT!**

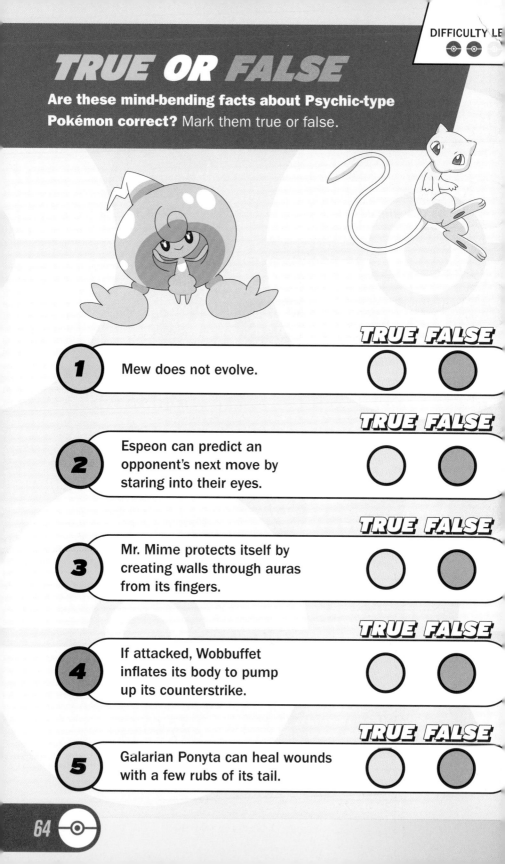

TRUE OR FALSE

Are these mind-bending facts about Psychic-type Pokémon correct? Mark them true or false.

TRUE FALSE

1 Mew does not evolve.   ◯ ◯

TRUE FALSE

2 Espeon can predict an opponent's next move by staring into their eyes.   ◯ ◯

TRUE FALSE

3 Mr. Mime protects itself by creating walls through auras from its fingers.   ◯ ◯

TRUE FALSE

4 If attacked, Wobbuffet inflates its body to pump up its counterstrike.   ◯ ◯

TRUE FALSE

5 Galarian Ponyta can heal wounds with a few rubs of its tail.   ◯ ◯

6 Galarian Rapidash has psychic power stored in its mane.

TRUE FALSE ◯ ◯

7 Psyduck is constantly bothered by pain in its head.

TRUE FALSE ◯ ◯

8 Hattrem attacks using fierce blows from the braids on its head.

TRUE FALSE ◯ ◯

9 When viewed through a microscope, Mew has small scales all over its body.

TRUE FALSE ◯ ◯

10 Galarian Rapidash is a Legendary Pokémon.

TRUE FALSE ◯ ◯

A TRIP TO HOENN!

The Hoenn region has held many adventures for our heroes. Check out these awesome facts!

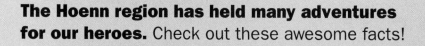

FACT 1

There are many different environments in the Hoenn region, from rain forests to deserts.

FACT 2

The waters off Slateport City in the Hoenn region are deep, filled with sunken treasure and wild Pokémon.

FACT 3

Contests such as the Battle Frontier Flute Cup and Pokémon Marine Athletic Race are held in the Hoenn region.

FACT 4

One time Ash and Goh investigated a whirling sandstorm in Mauville City. Inside was a sprawling desert and a Flygon!

FACT 5

They also visited Lavaridge Town when its hot springs were dried up by a layer of ice!

FACT 6

Goh has caught many Pokémon in the Hoenn region, such as Taillow, Trapinch, and Vibrava.

FACT 7

Goh has also failed to catch a few, including Wurmple and Luvdisc!

FACT 8

Ash and Goh researched the migration of Beautifly in the Hoenn region.

FACT 9

One of Goh's missions for Project Mew was to catch a wild Kingdra there.

FACT 10

There are many awesome Pokémon from the Hoenn region, such as the future-predicting Gardevoir and dancing Ludicolo.

FACT 11

Feebas may seem like a simple Fish Pokémon, but it evolves into the beautiful Milotic!

FACT 12

Goh once caught an Absol there, whose bow-like horn has a strong ability to detect danger.

LET'S ROLL WITH RAICHU!

Will these questions about the Electric-type Pokémon cause some static shock? Check them out!

1 What body part helps protect Raichu from its own high-voltage power?

2 What does a Pikachu need to evolve into a Raichu?

3 Where does Raichu store its energy?

4 What does it use to gather energy from the atmosphere?

5 Goh's Pikachu evolves into Raichu to save its friends, but from which enemies?

6 What's the name of the move where Raichu rubs its cheeks to create static energy, then rubs against its target to shock them?

WHO'S THAT POKÉMON?

DIFFICULTY LEVEL:

Cover this page with a sheet of paper and read one clue at a time. Count how many clues you read before correctly guessing the Pokémon.

1 This is a Fighting-type Pokémon.

2 It has enough stamina to keep running all through the night.

3 Ash received this Pokémon as an Egg before it hatched.

4 It becomes part of Ash's Pokémon family.

5 It can use waves called auras to see how others are feeling.

6 It evolves into Lucario.

The Pokémon is .... ,
and I needed .... clues.

HOW DID YOU DO? **TURN TO PAGE 93 TO FIND OUT!**

FACTS

YOU GOTTA KNOW!

PSYDUCK KINDNESS

This Psychic-type Pokémon has a caring side.

FACT 1

Psyduck is constantly bothered by headaches. The more its head hurts, the stronger its psychic power.

FACT 2

If Psyduck lets its strange power erupt, the pain in its head subsides for a while.

FACT 3

Psyduck can use intense psychic energy to overwhelm those around it.

FACT 4

Ash and Goh discovered that Psyduck doesn't like the cold. They met one who always wore a scarf!

FACT 5

The same Psyduck helped Cerise Laboratory researcher Chrysa when she felt sad and cold by loaning her its scarf.

FACT 6

Bonds between humans and Pokémon, like Chrysa and Psyduck, can provide emotional support for an eternity!

TRAINING AT SPEED!

Set a timer—how many of these Pokémon can you name in three minutes? Here we go!

DIFFICULTY LEVEL:

....

....

....

IN A FLASH!

Can you identify the Electric-type Pokémon? Look behind the lightning bolts for a hint, then write their number next to their name.

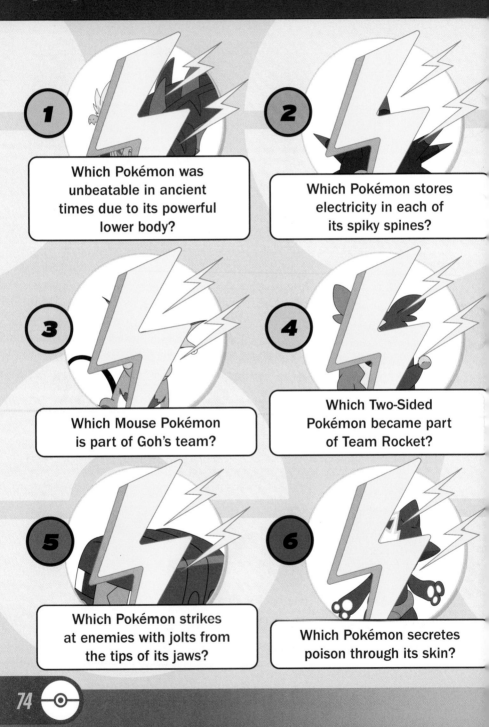

1 Which Pokémon was unbeatable in ancient times due to its powerful lower body?

2 Which Pokémon stores electricity in each of its spiky spines?

3 Which Mouse Pokémon is part of Goh's team?

4 Which Two-Sided Pokémon became part of Team Rocket?

5 Which Pokémon strikes at enemies with jolts from the tips of its jaws?

6 Which Pokémon secretes poison through its skin?

PICK THE RIGHT POKÉMON

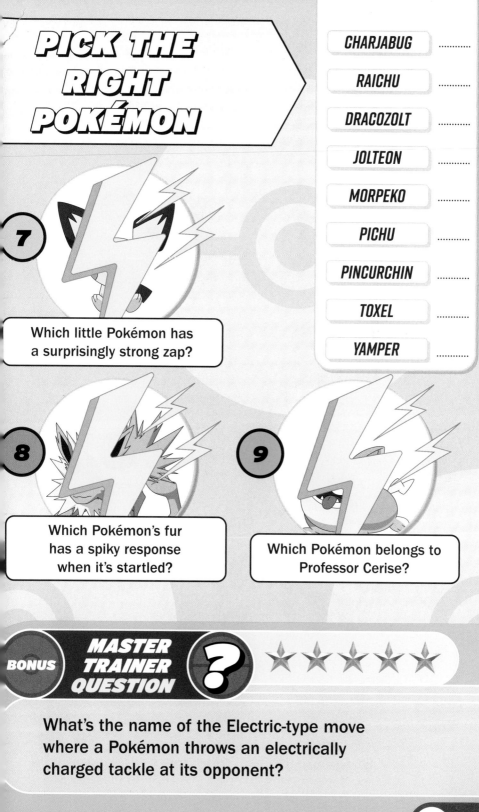

CHARJABUG ....

RAICHU ....

DRACOZOLT ....

JOLTEON ....

MORPEKO ....

PICHU ....

PINCURCHIN ....

TOXEL ....

YAMPER ....

7

Which little Pokémon has a surprisingly strong zap?

8

Which Pokémon's fur has a spiky response when it's startled?

9

Which Pokémon belongs to Professor Cerise?

BONUS | **MASTER TRAINER QUESTION** | **?** | ★ ★ ★ ★ ★

What's the name of the Electric-type move where a Pokémon throws an electrically charged tackle at its opponent?

HOW DID YOU DO? **TURN TO PAGE 95 TO FIND OUT!**

Questions 1–5

Which Pokémon is the **biggest**?

DIFFICULTY LEVEL:

1
- a. MORPEKO
- b. NICKIT
- c. CINDERACE

2
- a. GRAPPLOCT
- b. GALARIAN PONYTA
- c. INTELEON

3
- a. GRIMMSNARL
- b. GALARIAN FARFETCH'D
- c. IMPIDIMP

4
- a. ROOKIDEE
- b. SNORLAX
- c. RABOOT

5
- a. GALARIAN RAPIDASH
- b. DRACOVISH
- c. GALARIAN LINOONE

Small or big, these Galar region Pokémon can pack a punch!

Circle your answer for each question.

Questions **6–10**

Which Pokémon is the **smallest**?

6
- a SINISTEA
- b CORVIKNIGHT
- c DUBWOOL

7
- a FROSMOTH
- b SOBBLE
- c ORBEETLE

8
- a GALARIAN MEOWTH
- b DURALUDON
- c PERRSERKER

9
- a ROLYCOLY
- b DRIZZILE
- c EISCUE

10
- a STONJOURNER
- b TOXTRICITY
- c SILICOBRA

HOW DID YOU DO? **TURN TO PAGE 95 TO FIND OUT!**

GO, GO GRASS TYPES!

Can you catch four Grass-type Pokémon?
Circle and name them as you spot them.
Bonus points if you can name the others, too!

DIFFICULTY LEVEL:

GHOSTLY

FACTS

Get your spook on with these spine-tingling facts about Ghost-type Pokémon.

FACT 1

When Dragapult isn't battling, it keeps another Pokémon— Dreepy—in its horns!

FACT 2

Galarian Corsola absorbs the life forces of others through its branches.

FACT 3

If an opponent is licked by Haunter, they will soon shake from the poison.

Gastly has a gas-like body, so it can sneak into any place it likes!

FACT 4

FACT 5

Gengar is an expert at hiding in the shadows.

FACT 6

Galarian Yamask was formed when an ancient clay tablet was drawn to a vengeful spirit.

FACT 7

Runerigus is the evolved form of Yamask.

FACT 8

Rotom has a body made of plasma so it can inhabit all sorts of machines, like the Rotom Phone!

FACT 9

Dusclops's body is hollow—when it opens its mouth, it sucks everything in!

FACT 10

Sinistea was born when a lonely spirit possessed a cold, leftover cup of tea!

FACT 11

If someone touches the ectoplasmic body of Cursola, they'll become as stiff as stone!

Polteageist lives in antique teapots.

FACT 12

81

TRUE OR FALSE

Ready to battle with these Fighting-type facts?

Mark them true or false.

TRUE FALSE

1 When Clobbopus loses a tentacle, it cannot ever grow back.

TRUE FALSE

2 Sirfetch'd retires from combat when its leek withers.

TRUE FALSE

3 Grapploct lives on land and only enters water to battle.

TRUE FALSE

4 If Kubfu pulls its hair, its fighting spirit heightens.

TRUE FALSE

5 Lucario controls waves known as auras to take down opponents.

TRUE FALSE

6 Falinks is one Pokémon made up of ten individuals.

TRUE FALSE

7 Machoke is so powerful it has to wear a power-save belt.

TRUE FALSE

8 Gurdurr uses a metal beam as a weapon.

TRUE FALSE

9 Urshifu is feared for the speed of blows it can land on opponents.

TRUE FALSE

10 Zamazenta is a Warrior Pokémon.

ALL ABOUT MEW!

How well do you know the Mythical Pokémon that Goh vowed to catch?

1 What Pokémon type is Mew?

2 How tall is Mew?
a. 0'08"
b. 1'04"
c. 3'00"

3 Can Mew evolve?

4 Can you name one of Mew's moves?

5 What special skill does Mew possess that allows it to hide in the wild?

6 Legend has it that Mew will only show itself to those who are:
a. Ultra Class champions
b. Strong of mind
c. Pure of heart

7 Which Professor runs Project Mew?

8 Who was Goh with when he saw Mew for the first time?

9 Who was Mew battling when Goh first saw it?
a. Nidoking
b. Kangaskhan
c. Pikachu

10 The DNA of which Pokémon is said to be present in Mew?

11 What did Mew transform into when it saved Pikachu, Raboot, and Yamper from Team Rocket?

12 Which Pokémon was cloned from Mew?

HOW DID YOU DO? **TURN TO PAGE 96 TO FIND OUT!**

MASTER CLASS QUIZ

Battle challenge issued! These questions would be a test for any top Trainer. Let's see how many wins you can get from 1 to 20!

DIFFICULTY LEVEL:

Catch This!

1 Goh caught a Boldore in the Galar region. What does it evolve into?
a. Roggenrola
b. Gigalith
c. Geodude

2 True or false: Ash caught an Arctozolt in the Wild Area?

3 Goh caught a Bug- and Steel-type Pokémon in Unova that can crunch through rock with its mandibles. What's it called?

4 Goh once caught both a Diglett and Dugtrio, but which one did he keep?

5 Which member of Team Rocket caught a hungry Morpeko?

Got Some Moves!

6 Ash's Galarian Farfetch'd can slash at opponents, growing more powerful with each successive hit. What's that move?

7 In what move does Goh's Scizor slash at opponents by crossing its claws?
a. Metal Claw
b. Swords Dance
c. X-Scissor

8 Goh's Boldore can stick out its head and ram straight into an opponent. What's that move?

9 Which of Ash's Pokémon can use Draco Meteor, where it summons comets down from the sky onto its target?

10 Goh's Inteleon can surround its hands and feet with water and then hit its opponent with a full-force blast. What's that move?

Place to Place

11 In which region is the Castle of Chivalry?

12 True or False: Goh first met Grookey in Vermilion City, when he woke up to find it next to him.

○ ○

13 What is the domed area within the lab, where Ash's and Goh's caught Pokémon hang out?

14 In which region did Goh catch a Milcery that evolved into a Vanilla Cream Alcremie?

15 On Goh's first Project Mew trial mission, he and Ash visited the Desert Resort in which region?
a. Unova
b. Sinnoh
c. Johto

Pokémon Partners

16 Into which Pokémon does Sobble evolve?

17 Which evolution of Goh's Pokémon partner used Max Flare first?
a. Scorbunny
b. Raboot
c. Cinderace

18 True or False: Pikachu has never battled against Charizard.

○ ○

19 From which Trainer did Ash learn that his Lucario can Mega Evolve?
a. Bea
b. Gary
c. Korrina

20 Chloe took Eevee to meet which of its evolutions in Hoenn?

HOW DID YOU DO, TRAINER?

IT'S BEEN QUITE THE JOURNEY!

Check your answers on the next few pages to find out where your strengths are and where you stumbled. Did you beat any of the Master Trainer questions?

YOU CAN'T WIN EVERY BATTLE, BUT AS ASH SAYS, THE MOST IMPORTANT THING IS THAT YOU GOTTA TRY!

ANSWERS

PAGES 6-7
1. Scorbunny, **2.** Ninetales, **3.** Charizard,
4. Sizzlipede, **5.** Vulpix, **6.** Carkol, **7.** Centiskorch,
8. Cinderace, **9.** Arcanine
BONUS MASTER TRAINER QUESTION: Ho-Oh

PAGES 8-9
1. c, **2.** b, **3.** b, **4.** c, **5.** a, **6.** c, **7.** a, **8.** b
BONUS MASTER TRAINER QUESTION:
Kangaskhan

PAGES 10-11
1. Bulbasaur, **2.** Gyarados, **3.** Squirtle, **4.** Gengar,
5. Charmander, **6.** Snorlax, **7.** Rhydon,
8. Machamp
WHO GOT AWAY THIS TIME?
Magikarp, Lapras, Butterfree, Growlithe

PAGES 14-15
1. Inteleon, **2.** Thwackey, **3.** Silicobra, **4.** Perrserker,
5. Greedent, **6.** Dracovish, **7.** Clobbopus

PAGE 16
1. Fire, **2.** Galar, **3.** Raboot, **4.** Milotic, **5.** Pyro Ball,
6. Sobble

PAGE 17
1. Kanto, **2.** Johto, **3.** Hoenn, **4.** Unova, **5.** Sinnoh,
6. Kalos, **7.** Alola, **8.** Galar

ANSWERS

PAGES 18–19

1. b, **2.** c, **3.** a, **4.** c, **5.** a, **6.** c, **7.** b, **8.** b
BONUS MASTER TRAINER QUESTION:
Zweilous

PAGES 22–23

1. Galarian Farfetch'd, **2.** Galarian Stunfisk,
3. Galarian Linoone, **4.** Galarian Mr. Mime,
5. Galarian Rapidash, **6.** Galarian Zigzagoon,
7. Galarian Darmanitan

PAGES 24–25

1. Arctovish, **2.** Rillaboom, **3.** Obstagoon,
4. Sirfetch'd, **5.** Impidimp, **6.** Zamazenta,
7. Thievul, **8.** Morpeko.
The remaining Pokémon is Toxel.
BONUS MASTER TRAINER QUESTION:
Thievul

PAGES 26–27

1. False, it is West, **2.** True, **3.** True, **4.** False, it is
Goh's family, **5.** True, **6.** True, **7.** False, it sprays
poison, **8.** True, **9.** False, **10.** False, it is rare

PAGES 28–29

1. Ivysaur, **2.** Cinderace, **3.** Grookey, **4.** Inteleon,
5. Hattrem, **6.** Charizard, **7.** Machop
BONUS MASTER TRAINER QUESTION:
Flygon

ANSWERS

PAGE 32
1. Galar, 2. Its chest, 3. A Meteorite,
4. Eternamax, 5. Zacian, 6. Goh

PAGE 33
The Ice-type Pokémon is Snom.

PAGES 34–35
1. Hydro Pump, 2. Vine Whip, 3. Flamethrower,
4. Shadow Ball, 5. Aura Sphere, 6. Hyper Beam,
7. Razor Leaf, 8. Water Gun

PAGES 36–37
1. Charjabug, 2. Snom, 3. Blipbug, 4. Galvantula,
5. Centiskorch, 6. Orbeetle, 7. Butterfree,
8. Frosmoth, 9. Dottler

BONUS MASTER TRAINER QUESTION:
Scizor

PAGES 38–39
1. c (Nickit), 2. d (Greninja), 3. a (Impidimp),
4. b (Zigzagoon), 5. g (Zarude), 6. h (Obstagoon),
7. e (Linoone), 8. f (Morgrem)

PAGES 42–43
1. a, 2. c, 3. a, 4. c, 5. b, 6. a, 7. c, 8. b
BONUS MASTER TRAINER QUESTION:
Lugia

ANSWERS

PAGES 44–45

SOBBLE

DREDNAW

DRIZZILE

DRACOVISH

ARROKUDA

CHEWTLE

THE OTHERS

EISCUE

ARCTOZOLT

DRIZZILE

GRIMMSNARL

FALINKS

COPPERAJAH

DREEPY

PAGES 46–47

1. Snow, **2.** Espeon, **3.** Pink, **4.** It is poisonous, **5.** Flareon, **6.** Vaporeon, **7.** Jolteon, **8.** It will rain soon, **9.** Espeon, **10.** Leafeon, **11.** Their aroma, **12.** Sylveon

PAGES 52–53

1. Corviknight, **2.** Cramorant, **3.** Butterfree, **4.** Gyarados, **5.** Charizard, **6.** Corvisquire, **7.** Rookidee

BONUS MASTER TRAINER QUESTION:
Zapdos

ANSWERS

PAGES 54–55
1. b, **2.** a, **3.** b, **4.** c, **5.** b, **6.** a, **7.** c, **8.** a, **9.** b
BONUS MASTER TRAINER QUESTION:
Meowth

PAGES 56–57
1. c, **2.** a, **3.** a, **4.** c, **5.** c, **6.** c, **7.** b

PAGES 58–59
1. c, **2.** b, **3.** a, **4.** b, **5.** a, **6.** c, **7.** b, **8.** a
BONUS MASTER TRAINER QUESTION:
Vikavolt

PAGES 62–63
1. Barraskewda, **2.** Arcanine, **3.** Raboot,
4. Urshifu, **5.** Inteleon, **6.** Thievul, **7.** Greedent

PAGES 64–65
1. True, **2.** False, it's by reading air currents,
3. True, **4.** True, **5.** False, it uses its horn, **6.** False,
it's in the fur above its hooves, **7.** True, **8.** True,
9. False, it has fine hair, **10.** False

PAGE 68
1. Its tail, which grounds it, **2.** Thunder Stone,
3. In the electric pouches in its cheeks, **4.** Its tail,
5. Team Rocket, **6.** Nuzzle

PAGE 69
Riolu

ANSWERS

PAGES 72–73

GALARIAN MR. MIME

GALARIAN CORSOLA

GALARIAN STUNFISK

BARRASKEWDA

YAMPER

CHEWTLE

INTELEON

CINDERACE

URSHIFU

CORVIKNIGHT

TOXTRICITY

DRAGAPULT

THIEVUL

DREEPY

SOBBLE

EISCUE

SNOM

SIRFETCH'D

GRAPPLOCT

GROOKEY

SCORBUNNY

WOOLOO

NICKIT

SANDACONDA

ROOKIDEE

PERRSERKER

ZAMAZENTA

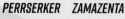

ANSWERS

PAGES 74–75

1. Dracozolt, **2.** Pincurchin, **3.** Raichu, **4.** Morpeko,
5. Charjabug, **6.** Toxel, **7.** Pichu, **8.** Jolteon,
9. Yamper

BONUS MASTER TRAINER QUESTION:
Spark

PAGES 76–77

1. c, **2.** c, **3.** a, **4.** b, **5.** b, **6.** a, **7.** b, **8.** a, **9.** a, **10.** b

PAGES 78–79

THWACKEY

ELDEGOSS

GOSSIFLEUR

FLAPPLE

THE OTHERS

FROSMOTH

WOOLOO

IMPIDIMP

CUFANT

APPLETUN

DOTTLER

DREEPY

FALINKS

GALARIAN PONYTA

95

ANSWERS

PAGES 82–83

1. False, it grows back easily, **2.** True,
3. False, it comes onto land to battle,
4. True, **5.** True, **6.** False, it is six parts, **7.** True,
8. True, **9.** False, it prefers one devastating blow,
10. True

PAGES 84–85

1. Psychic, **2.** b, **3.** No, **4.** Teleport, Fire Blast
or Transform, **5.** It can turn invisible, **6.** c,
7. Professor Amaranth, **8.** Chloe, **9.** a,
10. Every Pokémon! **11.** A Lugia, **12.** Mewtwo

PAGES 86–87

1. b, **2.** False, he caught a Dracovish, **3.** Durant,
4. Diglett, **5.** James, **6.** Fury Cutter, **7.** c,
8. Headbutt, **9.** Dragonite, **10.** Liquidation
11. Kalos, **12.** True, **13.** Cerise Park, **14.** Galar,
15. a, **16.** Drizzile, **17.** b, **18.** False, **19.** c,
20. Vaporeon